THIS CANDLEWICK BOOK BELONGS TO:

_____

_____

_____

_____

For Amelia and Ellen,
and all the rattletrap trips

P. R.

For Olivia Humphreys and Max Davies,
millennium babies

J. B.

Text copyright © 2001 by Phyllis Root
Illustrations copyright © 2001 by Jill Barton

First paperback edition 2004

The Library of Congress has cataloged the hardcover edition as follows:

Root, Phyllis.
Rattletrap car / Phyllis Root ;
illustrated by Jill Barton. — 1st ed.
p. cm.
Summary: Various disasters threaten to stop Poppa and the children
from getting to the lake in their rattletrap car, but they manage
to come up with an ingenious solution to each problem.
ISBN 0-7636-0919-6 (hardcover)
[1. Automobiles — Fiction. 2. Lakes — Fiction.] I. Barton, Jill, ill. II. Title.
PZ7.R6784 Rat   2001
[E] — dc21   99-057833

ISBN 0-7636-2007-6 (paperback)

4 6 8 10 9 7 5 3

Printed in China

This book was typeset in Kosmik Plain Two.
The illustrations were done in pencil and watercolor.

Candlewick Press
2067 Massachusetts Avenue
Cambridge, Massachusetts 02140

visit us at www.candlewick.com

Rattletrap Car

Phyllis Root ◆ illustrated by Jill Barton

CANDLEWICK PRESS
CAMBRIDGE, MASSACHUSETTS

Junie was hot.
Jakie was hot.
Even the baby was hot hot hot.
"Let's go to the lake," said
Junie and Jakie.
"Go!" said the baby.

"Oh dear," said Poppa. "I don't know if we can make it in our rattletrap car. It doesn't go fast and it doesn't go far."

"Please, please, please!" cried Junie and Jakie.

"Go!" cried the baby.

"All right," said Poppa. "We'll give it a try."

So he packed up a thermos full of
razzleberry dazzleberry snazzleberry fizz and
some chocolate marshmallow fudge delight.

Junie took her beach ball.
Jakie took his surfboard.
The baby took her
three-speed,
wind-up,
paddle-wheel boat.

Poppa turned the key,
brum brum, brum brum.

Clinkety clankety
bing bang pop!

They were off to the lake
in their rattletrap car.
They didn't go fast and
they didn't go far when

boomsssssssss.

The tire went flat.

"Never mind," said Junie.
"I know just what to do."

She put her beach ball on the car
and she stuck it on tight with
        chocolate marshmallow fudge delight.

Poppa turned the key,
brum brum, brum brum.

Lumpety bumpety
clinkety clankety
bing bang pop!

They were off to the lake
in their rattletrap car.
They didn't go fast and
they didn't go far when . . .

whumpety whomp!

The floor fell off.

"Never mind," said Jakie.
"I know just what to do."

He put his surfboard on the car
and he stuck it on tight with
chocolate marshmallow
fudge delight.

Poppa turned the key,
brum brum, brum brum.

Wappity bappity
lumpety bumpety
clinkety clankety
bing bang pop!

They were off to the lake
in their rattletrap car.
They didn't go fast and
they didn't go far
when . . .

spitter spitter sput!

The gas tank fell off.

"Never mind," said Poppa.
"I know just what to do."

He put the thermos full of razzleberry dazzleberry snazzleberry fizz on the car and he stuck it on tight with chocolate marshmallow fudge delight.

Poppa turned the key,
brum brum, brum brum.

Fizzelly sizzelly
wappity bappity
lumpety bumpety
clinkety clankety
bing bang pop!

They were off to
the lake in their
rattletrap car.

They didn't go fast and
they didn't go far when . . .

thunketa
thunk!

The engine fell out.

"Oh dear," said Jakie.
"Oh dear," said Junie.
"Oh dear," said Poppa.
"Oh dear, oh dear, oh dear, oh dear."

There they sat by the side of the road,
all broken down and hot hot hot,
almost to the lake in their
rattletrap car.

Junie shook her head.
Jakie shook his head.
Poppa shook his head.
The baby shook her
three-speed, wind-up,
paddle-wheel boat.

"Go," said the baby.
"Go, go, go."

"Do you think . . ." said Junie,
"that it just . . ." said Jakie,
"might work?" said Poppa.
"Go!" said the baby.

So they took the baby's boat
and put it on the car
and stuck it on tight
with chocolate marshmallow
fudge delight.

Poppa turned the key,
brum brum, brum brum.

Flippita fluppita
fizzelly sizzelly
wappity bappity
lumpety bumpety
clinkety clankety
bing bang

pop!

They were off to the lake in their rattletrap car!

They didn't go fast, but they did go far.
They made it to the lake in their rattletrap car!

Junie was cool. Jakie was cool.
Poppa and the baby were cool cool cool.
All day long they were cool at the lake
till the sun went down . . .

till the moon came up,
and they went

flippita fluppita

fizzelly sizzelly

wappity bappity

lumpety bumpety

clinkety clankety

bing bang pop!

all the way back home.